Around
the Corner

Kim Ablon Whitney

by

Kim Ablon Whitney

&

Caraneen Smith

#BarnBFF

Book 1: Around the Corner

Book 2: Hard to Catch

CONTENTS

CHAPTER ONE

COLLISION COURSE

"Canter around the corner. Then walk!" Kelly called out from the middle of the riding ring, a large sandy area surrounded by a bright white wooden fence. She was teaching Gemma Shu-Risso on her pony, Chewy. Gemma enjoyed their last few steps at the canter. Then the shiny brown pony slowed to a walk. Kelly said, "Good job. Give him a big pat."

Gemma didn't need to be told twice to pat Chewy. She loved her pony as much as he loved treats. Most ponies liked carrots and apples, but

Chewy liked sweets, too. Gemma still remembered the day he had reached over his stall door
and stolen a bite of her granola bar. Now everyone at Mangrove Equestrian Center, includ-
ing head trainer Kelly Van Beek, knew about
Chewy's love of granola bars. That's even how
he got his nickname.

"That's enough for today. You're in great
shape for the horse show next Saturday," Kelly
said.

When Gemma heard this, her coffee-colored
eyes sparkled. She grinned as brightly as the
Florida sunshine that afternoon. She thanked
Kelly for the lesson, then gave Chewy another pat. The bay pony sighed loudly as if he had
heard he was done, too. Sometimes Gemma
thought Chewy understood what people said.

Gemma walked Chewy into the middle of
the ring, swung her long legs over his back, and
dismounted. Her feet landed in a soft cloud of

sandy dust. She rolled up her leather stirrup straps just like she'd been taught in her first lesson five years ago. She knew a lot more about riding horses now, but it was still important to remember the basics.

She led Chewy toward the gate where other students and their ponies waited to enter the ring. First in line was a small girl with big blue eyes and curly brown hair gathered in a thick ponytail behind her helmet. Liv Gordon fidgeted with her reins, clearly eager to ride her new pony, Finn. Gemma had seen Liv around the barn, but they didn't usually ride at the same time and hadn't talked before.

Gemma paused as she walked by and said, "Hi! You're so lucky to have Finn. I saw him at horse shows with his old owner. He's such a good pony!"

"I know! I'm really excited to ride him," Liv said with a smile. She felt proud and lucky to own Finn. He was the first pony she had ever owned. Before she had only borrowed ponies from friends or leased them from her trainer. "I'm Liv, by the way. What's your name?"

"I'm Gemma and this is Chewy," she said. They talked for a few more moments before Gemma asked, "Are you showing next Saturday?"

Liv tensed a little. "Yes, but it's my first time showing Finn. I don't know if we will be a good team. So I am nervous."

Before Gemma could respond, Kelly's husky voice rang out, "Enough chit chat, you two!" Kelly called Liv into the ring to begin her lesson.

When Kelly called, students listened. She was basically a legend at Mangrove Equestrian. Everyone knew that she began riding even before she could walk. Her family had owned the farm for thirty years and she took over when her parents retired. While short and stout in appearance, she had command of any room she was in. Liv noticed her messy blonde hair always poked out of her sun visor.

Kelly's distinctly raspy voice came from years of calling out commands to her students from the middle of the ring. This included Liv, who got on Finn and began riding around the ring. Kelly gave her instructions as she rode along at the trot and then the canter.

When Kelly asked Liv to change direction, Liv suddenly noticed a rider on a large horse coming straight toward her. Liv pulled her right rein, then her left, but she didn't know which way to steer Finn around the horse. She braced herself as they nearly collided. Luckily the other horse and rider swerved away.

Kelly called Liv and Finn over. "Do you know how big that horse is? You almost got smooshed!" Kelly exclaimed.

"Well, Finn looks half his size," replied Liv.

Kelly continued, "Next time a big horse is about to trample you into a pony pancake, yell, 'INSIDE!' or 'OUTSIDE!' and then go around them."

Liv nodded. She asked eagerly, "Can we jump now?"

Kelly chuckled. "You always love to jump! Yes, go trot the cross-rail." She pointed to a small jump in the shape of an X made by its two poles crossing in the middle.

A cross-rail was the smallest kind of horse jump. Just the other day, Liv and her friends had jumped over these fences on foot without their ponies. But jumping with ponies was the most fun.

Liv trotted Finn toward the cross-rail. The fuzzy gray pony pricked his ears when he saw the jump. Liv got excited, too. Maybe too excited. Right as Finn went to take off, Liv leaned too far forward, pressing her weight on his neck. That made the jump feel a little bumpy.

"Don't get ahead of him," Kelly said. "Stay back in the saddle."

The next few times trotting the cross-rail were better.

"Great. Let's put together a little course for you," Kelly said.

Kelly and Liv were standing in the middle of the riding ring. All around them were colorful wooden fences to jump over. Sometimes riders would jump one or two, but Kelly wanted Liv and Finn to jump many of the fences in sequence. Kelly began to point out a series of fences. Liv memorized the order as Kelly spoke, "Start over the blue fence. Then around to the red jumps one after the other. Next come around over the green jumps. Finish over the yellow jumps riding toward the in-gate."

"This is simple. Just seven jumps," Liv

whispered to herself. It would be the same kind of course that Liv would have to jump at the horse show. Liv held her reins in one hand, while she traced the course in the air with her pointer finger. When she memorized it, she nodded at Kelly and gathered her reins.

Liv eased Finn from a trot to a canter and headed to the first jump. She felt he was on a good rhythm. Finn soared smoothly over it and Liv's heart flew with excitement. But on her way to the next fence, Finn turned too early. He was cutting the corner.

"C'mon, Finn!" she mumbled as she pulled his head toward the outside of the ring. She hoped her pony would straighten out. But this only made it worse. Liv realized they were aimed directly at the side of the jump, which held up the poles. If she didn't fix her direction, she and Finn might collide with the heavy wooden jump.

Liv's heart started to race. They were almost

at the jump. Should she keep going and risk a collision or circle to safety? The jump was coming closer and closer and closer. Liv held her breath and thought, "What if I crash?!"

CHAPTER TWO

A FUNNY LOOKING TREE

Liv could hear her own quick breaths. She heard the beating of Finn's hooves. What she did not hear was Kelly's voice. She hoped her trainer would call out, "Keep going!" Or, "Circle and try that again!" But Kelly was silent.

Finn's canter felt faster now. Time was running out. A split second away from the fence, Liv yanked hard on her inside rein and circled from the jump. She didn't want to have a bad jump and scare her pony. Or, even worse, hurt him if he crashed into the rails.

"Stop! Olivia Gordon, why did you do that?" Kelly's voice was stern. She even used Liv's full name. Liv was probably in big trouble.

Liv pulled up next to Kelly. "I knew I was crooked to the fence and I might hit the side. I thought you would tell me what to do."

Kelly raised her eyebrows. "It's important for you to solve problems on your own. Sometimes I will let you figure out what's happening as you ride. You're a very smart girl. And you know what I like to say, *smart girls are stable! You're* strong and secure and can make good decisions—even when things are happening fast as you ride around."

Kelly stepped over and put a hand on Liv's knee and continued, "But you should also never pull your pony away from a fence or it will become a bad habit. Finn will get you over any fence, but you have to trust him, okay? Try that again."

Liv bit her lip and nodded. This time she was determined to be firm around the corner, but Finn insisted on cutting the corner again! Liv grew frustrated.

Kelly called out, "Sit your bum in the saddle! Pull on your outside rein!"

Even though she wanted to circle again, she forced herself to trust Finn. Her foot barely scraped the side of the jump but Liv was proud they made it over the fence.

Yet when she slowed Finn to a walk, she felt a little gloomy. What if she couldn't learn to steer Finn in time for the horse show? She knew that at a horse show she couldn't collide or hit the side of the jump with her toe. The judges would not like that and she would feel embarrassed.

Liv's parents had bought Finn for her tenth birthday so she could move from the cross-rail classes into the next level. Suddenly she wasn't sure she was ready to move up to a higher class, even if the fences were only six inches taller. Liv thought she might be the only one in her classes who couldn't steer.

Kelly eyed Liv's face and sensed she was concerned. "Don't worry. We'll keep practicing until you and Finn learn how to work together as a team. I'll help you keep him from cutting the corner. Pretend I am a tree."

"A tree? How is a tree going to help me get around a corner?"

Kelly laughed. "Let me finish my instructions, silly."

Liv gave a sheepish smile.

Kelly continued, "I will stand in the corner, and you will have to go around me before you can turn to the first fence in the line."

"You're a funny looking tree, but I'll try it," Liv said.

"I think I am a great-looking tree!" Kelly laughed.

Kelly's trick worked. Liv was able to steer Finn around Kelly. As they jumped the rest of the course, Liv tried her best to pretend the "Kelly" tree was in each corner. Still, Finn only responded to her steering sometimes.

"That was better," Kelly said.

Liv knew it was better, but nowhere near her best. She was disappointed in herself and thinking ahead to the show. She wondered if she'd win any ribbons at all.

"Well, our time is up for this lesson. You made some good improvement with Finn. But it looks like we have something to work on," Kelly said. "It's not always easy when you get a new pony. You have to learn all of his quirks and he has to learn yours! We'll work more on staying straight tomorrow."

"Will I be okay by the horse show?" Liv asked.

"Of course. You're a good rider, you have a

great pony, and most importantly you have an awesome coach!" Kelly winked.

Even with Kelly's optimism, Liv wasn't confident after her tough lesson. She left the ring feeling unsettled. She even felt like she might cry. She contained her tears until she led Finn into his stall. She pressed her face into Finn's soft neck and let her tears mix with his silky fur. She didn't want anyone to hear her, but her breath caught and she sniffled loudly.

Two deep brown eyes appeared above the stall door and peered in from the barn aisle. A second later, Gemma popped her head into the stall, her almost jet-black hair whipping across her face. She cleared a strand of hair from her chin and asked, "Are you okay?"

CHAPTER THREE

SLIPPING SIDEWAYS

Liv jerked back from Finn, quickly wiping at her cheeks. She didn't know Gemma that well and she didn't like crying in front of older kids.

"I'm fine," Liv said with a quiver in her voice. Finn curled his head toward Gemma standing at the stall door. Gemma could see in his eyes that he was begging for her to come help his rider.

Liv looked up with red eyes and knew it was no use pretending. Plus Gemma seemed like a nice person. "Sorry . . . I . . . I . . . can't . . . ride . . . Finn," she blurted through a few more sniffles.

Having cried after hard lessons many times before, Gemma knew just how Liv felt.

Stepping into the stall, Gemma asked Liv, "You've only had him a few weeks, right?"

Liv nodded and Gemma continued, "It takes a while to get to know a pony. What happened?"

"I almost crashed and he cut almost every corner except when there was a tree."

"A tree?" Gemma looked confused, but curious.

"Oh. Kelly pretended to be a tree and I had to ride around the tree." Saying this made Liv smile a tiny bit.

Gemma chuckled. "That reminds me of my first rides on Chewy, too. I also had a hard time. One time, Kelly even tried putting balloons around the ring to help me steer. Chewy spooked and almost bucked me off!"

Liv let out a weak giggle. "I'm glad she didn't try balloons with me!"

"Kelly comes up with some pretty crazy ideas," Gemma said.

Gemma was making Liv feel a little better. Liv could feel her shoulders relax and the pit in her stomach fade away. Still, she didn't know if she could get her courses smoothed out by the horse show.

Gemma gave her a warm smile. "You've still got time. I bet you'll get it." With this, Finn nudged them to move along. He seemed to know Liv was feeling better and it was time for his hay. Like many horses, he preferred to eat his dinner alone.

Stepping outside of the stall, Gemma announced, "I think I'm only a year older than you. I'm eleven."

"I'm ten," Liv said.

"You wanna see if maybe Kelly will let us have a lesson together?"

"OMG, yes!" Liv exclaimed.

Gemma whipped out her cell phone and text-ed Kelly, *CAN I PLS LESSON W LIV?*

*F*rom down the barn aisle, they heard a ping. Kelly glanced at her phone, then scanned the aisle. She sighted Liv and Gemma and called out, "Seriously, Gemma? Did you forget you have feet and legs? Next time come and ask me instead of text-yelling at me!" But then she quickly agreed they would make good lesson buddies.

✻

The day of the girl's first lesson together, Gem-ma started to put the bridle on Chewy. But first, she put her head next to his face and snapped a selfie with him for her Instagram. Her parents didn't let her use many apps, but all the barn kids liked to share photos of their ponies on In-sta.

With a few taps the picture popped onto her feed along with many heart emojis and the caption, *##*BAE*##* about to ride! #thecutest. She knew she'd get lots of likes and comments. Chewy was so cute. How could anyone not love him?

Gemma's family had owned Chewy for many years and he was part of the family. He was a beautiful dapple bay, with big, dark eyes and a white blaze that ran slanted downward across his face. Along with Gemma's older sister, Skylar, Chewy had taught many children how to ride. That didn't mean he was easy to ride, but he was a good teacher.

The girls finished preparing to ride and headed toward the ring. As the two girls approached a small step-ladder to get on their ponies, Gemma turned to Liv and said, "This is going to be so much fun!"

"I hope so. I haven't done many lessons with friends, mostly just by myself," Liv replied.

"It's much better than having a lesson alone because sometimes you get more time to rest. Plus, you can learn from each other." Gemma swung her leg over Chewy's back, gently sitting herself down into the saddle. Dangling her legs down, she tapped her ankles against the metal of her stirrup irons. She asked, "Are my stirrups the same length?"

Liv was happy to help Gemma, especially after Gemma had made her feel better the day before. She looked closely at Gemma's feet to tell whether they reached the same spot on Chewy's sides. She concluded, "The right one is a little longer."

"That's what I thought. I hate when I feel like one stirrup is longer than the other," Gemma said.

"I hate that, too," Liv agreed.

Kelly soon greeted the girls and promised they would have to work extra hard together. Gemma and Liv exchanged glances that seemed to say, *uh-oh*. Liv looked again over at Gemma and Chewy and wished she were a year older. Then she would be more experienced like them. And she would already have done horse shows with Finn. And she would know whether she would do well.

Gemma, meanwhile, started trotting Chewy. Only a moment later Kelly called out the dreaded phrase, "Sit the trot, girls!"

Usually riders do an up-down motion called posting where they switch between sitting and then standing up in the stirrups to the rhythm of the pony's trot. The sit-trot required Gemma to sit all of the trot steps without standing up. Sitting trot was actually harder to do than posting to the trot.

Chewy's trot was really bumpy. Gemma was

tall for an eleven-year-old and squeezed her long legs extra tight. She tried to keep her bum in the saddle. It was hard to keep herself from bouncing. Chewy pinned his ears back in anger at the bump-bump of Gemma's bum hitting the saddle hard.

Suddenly, Gemma noticed that with every step she seemed to be slipping sideways. She scrunched her legs as tight as she could but she was still tilting sideways off of Chewy.

"Oh no! My girth!"

She had forgotten to make her girth tighter to the saddle after getting on.

If she didn't think fast, her saddle would end up under her pony's belly and Gemma would drop head first into the dirt!

CHAPTER FOUR

WHO'S THE BOSS

Just as Gemma reached for her reins to stop Chewy, the saddle slipped sideways. Gemma quickly grabbed Chewy's mane and swung her legs over his back, dismounting like an Olympic gymnast. Landing on her feet, she ran a few steps alongside Chewy and pulled him up. Chewy turned his head and gave her an annoyed look. *Silly kid,* he seemed to say.

Gemma saw Liv with her mouth wide open in surprise.

Kelly, who was instructing Liv, turned

around and saw Gemma off her pony. "What in the world?" She lowered her voice, "Chewy, you naughty boy, did you buck off Gemma?"

Chewy did have a mischievous streak and occasionally bucked, but that day he was being a good boy.

"Er, um, no. Don't be mad at Chewy. It's my fault. My girth was too loose and my saddle slipped," Gemma said, her face flushed with embarrassment. "I did an emergency dismount."

Kelly frowned at Gemma. "It's a good thing you're so cool under pressure. I'm glad you're okay. But maybe if you weren't so busy taking selfies and chatting with your friends, you might remember to tighten your girth. Safety first. It won't happen again, right?"

Gemma nodded and promptly tightened her girth before hopping back on.

"Okay girls, back to business."

Liv was excited as usual, but a little tense

after her last lesson. As they trotted around Liv didn't notice her hands were balled tightly around the reins and pulling on Finn's face. He lay his ears flat back in annoyance and Kelly noticed. "Liv, try to relax and not pull so hard on Finn's mouth."

After working at the canter in both directions, Kelly decided they were ready to jump. Gemma wanted to be extra good and show Kelly she was a smart, responsible rider after her mishap.

"Gemma, you go first," Kelly said. "Liv, come stand Finn over here." Kelly pointed to a spot in the ring where Liv wouldn't be in the way of any jumps.

Gemma started riding Chewy last year. She had learned how to ride him well, but she knew that learning never ends when it comes to ponies.

In fact, Gemma didn't notice Chewy going too slow. Kelly soon reminded her. "Chewy's being a slug! He's not on a vacation! Keep him going," Kelly told her. "You can't take your leg off him for one second."

As Liv waited, her mind wandered. When Kelly mentioned a vacation, Liv pictured Finn on the beach with big sunglasses and a bucket hat. She had a big imagination and funny images often popped into her mind. She wondered if this happened to other people or just to her. She hadn't told anyone about it.

Gemma finished her course and was out of breath, but it went well. She leaned down and gave Chewy a big hug around his neck.

Kelly praised her, "That was good. Just do that a few more times at the show, and you'll be bringing home more blue ribbons."

Gemma beamed.

Liv was happy for Gemma but wished Kelly would say that to her. Her mind pictured flowing blue ribbons pinned to Finn's bridle. But she knew that was only in her mind. She was still unsure that she and Finn were good partners.

"Okay, Miss Liv. Your turn. You know what I'm going to say to you, don't you?"

"Keep Finn from cutting corners."

"Exactly."

Liv picked up a canter and headed to the first jump. Before they reached the corner, Finn crooked his head sideways and began to make a beeline for the jump. Liv was certain Finn was disobeying her on purpose! She could feel her ears turn hot with anger. Finn took the jump awkwardly.

She told herself to *KEEP CALM AND RIDE ON*. That's what the framed poster on the tack room wall said. Liv knew she had to pull herself together, but the next two jumps were just as bad. She felt very discouraged.

After the last jump she came back to a walk.

She slumped her shoulders. "I was trying," she told Kelly.

"Yes, you were," she said and paused to think. After a moment, Kelly's eyes lit up and she looked excitedly at Liv. "You know what? I think I've just discovered something about Finn. Can you guess what?"

"Um. He's got a pink nose?" Liv wasn't sure what Kelly was getting at.

"Nope. It's something you and Finn have in common."

Gemma piped up, "I know! I know! They're both ten years old."

Kelly shook her head. "That's true, but it's something else."

Liv could tell Kelly was bursting to tell her. "You know who else loves to jump, just like you? Finn!"

Liv had noticed how excited Finn felt when

they began to jump. His ears would prick forward and his canter would quicken.

Kelly explained, "He's really intelligent. I think he's trying to look for the next jump before you turn. You'll have to teach him to wait. He has to know you're the boss. Right now he thinks he's the boss."

Liv imagined herself sitting behind a big fancy desk in an office on the top floor of a huge building. She wore slim black pants and a flowing blouse like her mom wore to work. She imagined Finn dressed in human clothes coming out of the office elevator, his white hair poking out of the pant legs.

"Earth to Liv! Are you there?" Kelly said. Liv snapped back to attention as Kelly continued, "Remember, you are the boss! Go try again."

Liv walked past Gemma feeling uncertain that she could do it. She whispered, "Got any pointers before I try again?"

Gemma simply raised a fist and declared, "You can do it!"

Liv was glad Gemma believed in her. "Okay, Finn, let's go. I know we both love to jump, but you have to wait for me," Liv said quietly to her pony. Finn's ears flicked back as she said it, and Liv wondered if he understood. As they cantered on, Liv was more determined than ever. She didn't let Finn look early toward the jump. Liv was surprised that he arched his neck high. It seemed like he was suddenly proud to be Liv's pony.

Kelly shouted with glee, "He's listening to you now. Way to be the boss!"

Liv rode as tall and proud as ever, calmly watching the fence approach through Finn's fuzzy ears. She was coming at the jump perfectly straight! Liv could feel herself getting excited. Liv and Finn cruised around the ring finishing the course.

"Excellent!" Kelly exclaimed. "That's your best course yet with Finny!"

Kelly was pleased that both girls had ended their lesson well. Gemma pulled alongside Liv and said, "That was hashtag AWESOME. We are going to dominate the horse show." She paused and continued with a wry smile, "As long as you are Finn's boss and I remember to keep my saddle on!"

Liv laughed. "Thanks for cheering me on. I needed that."

CHAPTER FIVE

THE SHOW MUST GO ON

Gemma and Liv walked their ponies and chatted for a while. Both girls were excited to learn about each other.

"OMG, I love Nickelodeon, too. The shows are so funny! Wait, so you actually met Jace Norman? For reals?" Gemma asked.

Gemma was generally pretty chill, but anything about the young actor Jace Norman made her head spin. In a good way.

"For reals. Yeah, last year my family went on vacation to California. We visited Hollywood.

We were walking around some shops and I looked up and there he was. He walked by with some grownups. I was like, WHAAAAA?!" Liv confessed she almost didn't believe it was him. "He looked a little different from TV. He was wearing a baseball cap."

"Okay, so technically, you haven't met. But still. I would've freaked out!" Gemma blurted. "He's so cute on TV. Was he cute IRL?"

Liv nodded. "Yaaaaaassssss!"

Both girls began giggling.

Chewy got bored easily and liked to nibble on the reins as they walked. He then reached over and playfully nipped at Finn to entertain himself. But Finn wasn't feeling playful. So he made a short little squealing noise and pinned his ears back at Chewy.

Liv said, "Our ponies aren't best friends, I guess. But I'm glad we're having fun."

Both girls dismounted next to the barn and

brought the ponies inside for their post-lesson grooming. They brushed them until their coats gleamed.

Soon enough, it was time to go home. Liv's father arrived to pick her up and greeted her with a big hug saying, "How's my little peanut?"

Liv squirmed away and rolled her eyes. "Dad! You promised!"

She didn't like her dad using her pet name in front of her friends. She quickly changed the subject. "This is Gemma Shu-Risso," Liv told her dad. "She's the one I'm having lessons with."

"Nice to meet you," Mr. Gordon said as he stretched his hand out to Gemma.

"The pleasure is all mine," Gemma said doing her best adult imitation. Then she looked at Liv and they burst into giggles for no obvious reason. Gemma liked to be a little silly. Most adults liked that she was funny, or as her mom said, *she had personality.*

Mr. Gordon wasn't sure what the two girls thought was funny, but he smiled seeing his daughter happy with her new friend. "Okay, Liv. Time to go."

The girls said goodbye. On her way out of the barn, Liv told her father she wanted to say goodnight to Finn. She leaned her face close to the bars of his stall door and called his name in a sing-song voice. He picked up his head and brought his nose to her face and nuzzled her. His warm, soft nose against her cheek was the best feeling in the whole world. Her heart swelled as she looked at her pony. Her pony! She *actually* owned a pony IRL!

As Liv turned to leave, Gemma called out one last time. "Hey Liv, wait!" She skipped down the aisle of the barn. "Do you have Insta? I wanna follow you."

"I have an account. I can't post, but my parents let me follow my friends," Liv said.

"Great, you can follow me and Chewy. He's *Insta-famous,*" Gemma said with pride. "I'm almost to three hundred followers."

"No way!" Liv wished she could share photos. Her parents didn't want her using her phone too much. Everyone else did it and sometimes Liv wished her parents weren't so strict. But they just got her Finn and she'd rather have a pony than more time on her phone!

The two girls exchanged Insta accounts and Liv jogged happily over to her dad's car and headed home.

❋

Gemma's mom was ten minutes late. Gemma had gotten used to waiting around lately. Since her parents divorced things had been a little disorganized as the family figured out their new routine.

During the school week, Gemma and her sister, Skylar, lived with their mom in Palm Palisades, the same suburb where Mangrove Equestrian was located. Every other weekend, they headed to their dad's condo. It was in a high-rise overlooking the city of Timu Beach. Even though Gemma had to go back and forth between her parents' places, she was grateful they were only about twenty minutes apart.

As Gemma got into the back seat, Mrs. Shu-Risso asked how the lesson went. Gemma clicked on her seatbelt and replied, "It was great. I really like Liv. She'll be showing in the same class at the horse show."

"That's wonderful, honey," her mom said. Her phone pinged and Mrs. Shu-Risso looked at a text message. She tapped a reply and explained, "Hadley's baby shower is right around the corner. I'm in charge of the food."

Hadley was her mother's best friend from

college. She sent Gemma and her sister the best birthday gifts. Now, she was finally having a baby of her own and Gemma's mother was going all out.

"I thought you were coming to the horse show?" Gemma asked, her voice concerned.

"Don't worry, your dad will go with you," said Mrs. Shu-Risso.

They drove along for a few minutes in silence. Gemma's thoughts wandered back to her parents' divorce, and she asked, "Hey, Mom, are you going to keep Dad's last name, or just go by Shu again? And will Dad just be Dr. Risso now?"

Her mom thought a moment. "We're still working that out, honey. For now we'll be the Shu-Rissos like we've always been."

It was nice to think that at least in name they were still one family.

Gemma pulled out her phone and tapped a message to her dad, *can't wait till the show, can* *we stop for ice cream after? T*he Shu-Rissos loved the nearby Coconut Ice Cream Hut and its seventy-three delicious flavors.

Dr. Shu-Risso didn't write back. He was probably in surgery. He operated on people who had been in car crashes and other accidents. That night, her dad finally texted back, *Hi Gem, I've got to talk to your mom about the show, love you little girl. G*emma didn't like the sound of that. Usually he was as excited as she was.

After a few minutes, her mom knocked on her door and poked her head in. "Hey, there, you about ready for bed?"

"I guess," Gemma said. "Did you talk to Dad about the show?"

Her mom saw Gemma had been laying out her clothes for the horse show and her face turned a little sad. "So we've got a little problem . . ." her mom began. "Dad and I had a mix-up with our schedules. He has to work and I can't miss Hadley's baby shower."

"No!" Tears sprouted quickly in Gemma's eyes. She had been looking forward to this horse show for weeks. "I can't miss the show!"

Gemma was cool-headed about nearly everything, but she hated to miss any day at the barn and especially a horse show. The recent changes in her family had sometimes made her home feel uncomfortable, but the barn was always a safe, happy place. She also loved Chewy more than anything. He had helped her through some tough days with his bright face and endearing personality.

Gemma threw herself onto her bed, buried her face in her unicorn pillow and wailed, "I can't miss the show!"

"I know this stinks," her mom said, putting a hand on her back.

"If you knew how much it stinks, you'd do something!" Gemma said.

Mrs. Shu-Risso sighed. "I'll see what I can do, but I can't promise we can make it work."

Gemma went to sleep that night unsettled. She had been practicing with Chewy for weeks. She felt like she was letting Kelly down after their hard work together. And now she was extra excited to show with her new friend, Liv. What if she couldn't go to the horse show?

CHAPTER SIX

BEST. AUNT. EVER.

L iv arrived at the barn in a great mood, still excited after her lesson with Gemma. She stuck her head into Kelly's office and asked what kind of a workout she should give Finn.

"I think the ponies need a little rest. Just give them a light ride, enough to stretch their legs and all their muscles. And don't forget to graze them for a treat after you ride!" Kelly smiled and then went back to doing paperwork.

Gemma came after Liv had already started riding Finn, but soon she and Chewy joined them in the ring. The girls rode for about twenty minutes, then went and walked in the big grassy field behind the barn so the ponies could cool down.

"I'm packed for the show," Liv said. "What about you?"

"Um, I guess . . . yeah," Gemma said. Her voice was dull.

Liv wasn't sure how to respond. Something was off. She was used to Gemma being more up-beat.

They walked some more, watching a few thunder clouds build in the distance. "Maybe we should get off before the storm comes," suggested Liv. Both girls knew that it could go from sunny to stormy very quickly in Florida.

They walked back to the ring. Since Gemma wasn't talkative, Liv let her mind wander. She stared up at the puffy clouds and thought she saw a horse shape, white just like Finn.

Then she imagined Finn flying upward into the clouds. He was after all named after a bird. His full name was Silver Finch.

Both girls dismounted. Gemma forgot to run up her stirrups like she always did. They were dangling at Chewy's side. As they began to walk, one of the stirrups started to catch on a branch poking out from a nearby bush. It could have startled Chewy.

"Gemma! Your stirrup is caught," Liv squeaked.

Gemma whipped her head around and saw her mistake. "Oh my goodness! First the girth, now this . . . What's wrong with me? Seriously, IDK."

Except she did know exactly what was wrong. Before she was forgetful because of her selfies. Today she was upset about the show. Her mom hadn't found anyone to take her. Gemma asked her dad if he could switch his work hours. He could, but then he'd have to miss their big Memorial Day party instead. Skylar would be really angry if that happened.

Liv thought Gemma seemed sad but she didn't want to say so. Instead Liv said, "You seem kind of, I don't know, distracted today." Then she tried to lighten the mood, joking, "Did Chewy step on your phone or something?"

Gemma hadn't posted one single Insta photo since the previous evening.

Gemma didn't want to tell anyone yet, but she finally confessed, "I might not be able to go to the show."

"What? Why?" Liv asked.

"It's a mix up. My mom is going away for the weekend. She can't change her plans. My dad is working all weekend."

Liv's stomach tightened a little. It made her nervous to think about showing without her new friend. Gemma had already helped her in just one lesson together.

"I'm not sure I even want to show if you can't," Liv told Gemma.

"Of course you do. That's crazy."

Liv wished she could invite Gemma to stay with her for the weekend. But they weren't close enough friends yet. Besides, Liv's parents only let her have sleepovers during the summer and school wasn't out for another month.

Liv sighed and responded, "It won't be nearly as much fun without you."

"I'm still hoping I can find a way to go," Gemma said. It was the first show of the Shark Island Show Series and Gemma badly wanted to win a year-end award. Riders had to go to all the horse shows and earn points by winning ribbons. Gemma continued, "You know all the kids who get year-end awards get a huge stuffed-animal shark! But if I miss the first horse show, I probably don't have a chance."

✳

Gemma was quiet on the drive home. She knew time was running out. She had to find someone to take her to the show—and fast. On Friday morning, her mom would make the five-hour drive to Hadley's house. If Gemma went with her mom and Skylar, she would have to skip school. Usually she would have been happy to get out of school, but not this time.

At eight o'clock she was still trying to finish her math homework. She mumbled numbers as she worked, "964 divided by 8, 8 goes into 9," then paused and a brilliant idea popped into her head. She exclaimed out loud, "AUNT MIMI!" The idea struck like lightning! Why hadn't it occurred to her earlier? Her father's younger sister, Noemi Risso, was the most spontaneous person she knew. And she rode horses, too. If anyone would understand how important the show was to her, it would be Mimi.

Mimi lived in Virginia with her young daughter Jasmine, who she adopted last year from Guatemala. It might be hard for Mimi to get away for the weekend. It was a longshot but Gemma had to try it. She thought about having her dad call her, but then decided to call herself. Mimi always had a hard time saying no to Gemma.

Gemma pulled out her phone and hit the Facetime button. After a few beeps, Mimi's grinning face popped onto the screen. "Gemmy-Gem-Gemmers! How's my favorite niece?" She quickly corrected herself, "Er, ONE of my favorite nieces. Don't tell Sky I said that."

Gemma chuckled. She loved her aunt. Just as Gemma was about to reply, her aunt's phone appeared to take a massive somersault. She heard her tiny cousin squeal with naughty delight.

Mimi's voice screeched, "Jazzy! Jazzy! Give that back." A moment later, the phone righted itself. Mimi placed Jasmine on her lap and pointed at the screen. "Look, Jazzy, there's your cousin Gemma!"

"Hi, Jazz!" Gemma waved to her squirming cousin.

"GUMMA!" Jasmine blurted loudly. She was only eighteen-months and just learning to talk.

Gemma could hardly get past the pleasantries before she asked, "I was wondering what you are doing this weekend?"

Mimi raised one eyebrow. "Why?"

Gemma meant to explain things slowly but the words tumbled out of her mouth. "I've got a horse show this weekend but Mom has to go to Hadley's baby shower and Dad has to work and they got it all totally mixed up so now I have to miss my show and go with Mom to the shower but I want to ride with my friend and I can't miss this show or I won't win a shark—"

"Dear me! Take a breath, child," Mimi said, cutting her off.

"Please, Auntie Mimi." Gemma's eyes widened and she made her best puppy dog face. "Is there any way you could take me to the show on Saturday?"

Gemma waited, breathless.

"Saturday? That's a big ask. It's three days away." Mimi hesitated a moment before bursting into a huge, toothy smile. "But yes! You know I love an adventure. We'll catch the Friday afternoon flight."

Gemma was stunned. She couldn't believe it. Then it felt like fireworks were shooting all over her body. She began jumping up and down, and shrieked, "Thank you so much, Auntie Mimi!"

After saying goodnight to Auntie Mimi, Gemma immediately swiped through pictures on her phone. She found one of her aunt standing next to Chewy last summer. She quickly posted it onto Insta.

#flashback BEST.AUNT.EVER. xoxo #andbestpony #seeyousaturday #horseshow

*P*lus a zillion heart-emojis.

A few miles away, Liv couldn't fall asleep. She snuck out of bed and grabbed her phone to check Insta. Her heart leapt seeing the first photo, a bright bay pony with a blaze. Beside him was a woman with the biggest smile she'd ever seen.

Liv tapped the heart button and smiled to herself, before finally dozing off to sleep.

CHAPTER SEVEN

READY, SET, GO!

The day before a horse show was almost as exciting as the horse show itself. Gemma couldn't wait to get to the barn. And even better, she couldn't wait to see Auntie Mimi that evening. The last few hours of her day at school dragged by.

Seconds after the final bell, Gemma burst through the school doors, first out.

Her dad was waiting and they drove to the barn. "I still don't know how in the world you convinced Mimi to come for the weekend. But

I'm glad I'll get to spend some time with her, too. So good work, kiddo," Dr. Shu-Risso said.

As they pulled into the driveway at Mangrove Equestrian, Gemma's hand rested on her seatbelt buckle. She was ready to bolt out of the car. Her dad caught sight of her eager face in the rearview mirror. "Okay honey, I'm going to head to the airport and get Mimi. She'll pick you up in a few hours."

"Perfect. Thanks, Daddy!" The car came to a stop, Gemma clicked off her seatbelt, pecked her dad on the cheek, and threw open the car door. "Bye!"

Liv greeted Gemma. "What took you so long? What time do you get out of school? We get out at 2:15."

Liv went to Palm Palisades Public Elementary, but Gemma attended a private school for girls, Hickory Bay Academy.

"Lucky! We don't get out until 2:45pm at my school," Gemma replied.

"I guess I'm glad I don't go to your school," Liv said. "Although I hear Hickory Bay has a really cool climbing wall in the gym."

Gemma loved the wall. She promised they'd go climb it sometime, but first they had a show tomorrow.

The barn was bustling with activity that afternoon as everyone got ready to show. A young boy named Landon Garcia was going. He was around the same age as Gemma and Liv, but he only began riding a few months earlier. It was his first horse show. Older riders were also going: teenagers, twenty-somethings, and a few riders that were the same age as the girls' parents.

The girls got on their ponies for their final lesson before tomorrow.

"Okay, who's ready for a horse show?!" Kelly's voice rang out from across the ring.

Both girls simultaneously waved a hand and shouted back, "MEEEEE!"

Kelly pumped her fist and exclaimed, "It's gonna be great, girls. I just know it."

Gemma was thrilled. She had done three horse shows last summer, so she felt like an old pro. Liv smiled and pretended to be thrilled, but worries kept popping into her mind. What if Finn wouldn't listen to her? He'd been better since her bad lesson, but what if he forgot what he had learned?

Thankfully, the lesson went smoothly for both girls and their ponies. Afterwards, they brought the ponies to the wash rack behind the barn. When Kelly wasn't looking, Liv and Gemma sprayed the hose at each other playfully. Usually that wasn't a good thing to do near a pony, but neither pony was scared of the hose.

Chewy, true to his name, actually liked to chew on the hose and slurp water right from it.

Just as Liv sent a squirt in Gemma's direction, Kelly's head popped out from the barn. "Hey, you two. Stop squirting each other. That's not allowed, remember?" The girls secretly snuck a few more squirts, holding in their giggles so Kelly wouldn't hear them. But Kelly peered out again and warned they couldn't show if they kept it up. Both hoses immediately stopped being squirted.

They got to work bathing their ponies so they were clean and shiny for the show. Liv looked at Finn. He looked like a blank white canvas—a white canvas with a huge brown splotch in the middle. One of Finn's worst habits was lying in his doodies. A lot of ponies only lay down for a few minutes each night. Finn liked to sprawl out for hours and often chose the dirtiest place in his stall. Liv was always grossed out by the brown stain on his coat. It took a lot of elbow grease and shampoo to make it disappear.

As she dried him off, she said sternly, "Now don't you dare go getting dirty again tonight!"

Gemma called over, "That's why I like having a bay pony!" Chewy's dark colored fur hid dirt and stains.

Liv pretended to cover Finn's ears and turned to Gemma. "Don't tell Finn, but white ponies are the worst!"

Finn seemed to hear anyway. He shook his head and shoved his nose into the nearby soap bucket, knocking it over. He lifted his head and his pink nose was covered in soap bubbles.

"Look at him!" Liv said, laughing.

"OMG, that's gotta go on Insta. Get your phone!" Gemma held Finn while Liv pulled out her phone.

Liv wasn't sure her parents would be okay if

she posted a photo to her Insta. Maybe as long as she wasn't in the photo, her parents would think that was okay.

Liv perched herself in front of Finn and snapped a bunch of quick pictures. "These are so cute!"

Just as she went to get up, Finn blew a massive sneeze right in her face. Soap suds blew all over both girls. They doubled over, laughing.

Still giggling, the girls then led their ponies to the back field to graze and dry off. The golden rays of the late afternoon Florida sunshine blazed down and helped dry the ponies' fur. The girls lost track of time chatting and watching their ponies nibble at the green grass. Soon the shadows from the palm trees edging the field grew long and the girls finally took the ponies back to their stalls.

Liv and Gemma sat down on a storage trunk.

They looked through the photos of Finn with the soap suds and picked their favorite. Gemma expertly showed Liv how to pick a filter.

"I'm not sure I should post it," Liv said. "My parents might be mad."

"It's just a photo of your pony," Gemma said. "Why would they mind that?"

"I guess they wouldn't," Liv said.

"Don't post it if you don't want to," Gemma said. "I don't want you getting in trouble either."

Liv looked at the photo again. It was so cute! "I think it will be fine." She added her own caption and pressed post. *funny Finny today! #ICYMI #blowingbubbles #bathtime #ponylife.*

"That is legit SO cute," Gemma said.

"I love it. I hope my parents will let me keep it posted," Liv said.

The girls spent the next hour packing and organizing for the show. It would be a really busy day. The better prepared they were, the smoother the show would go. Plus, they would have to get up very early the next morning.

By the end of the afternoon, the ponies were clean and the girls were dirty. It was good Liv had worn her old jeans because they were stained brown. Her fingers were also purple from the whitening shampoo she used on Finn.

Gemma had a yellowish-green mark on her shirt from where Chewy had slobbered on her. Gemma's lower legs and socks got so wet that the water seeped into her boots and she'd been walking around with damp toes.

Both girls were also dog-tired. When Liv got home at dusk, all she wanted to do was go to sleep. She crashed on the sofa and began watching Nickelodeon while her parents cooked dinner together. Later, she got up and walked to the kitchen to see when the food would be done.

Her parents were huddled close together, looking at her mom's phone. Both parents looked up at the same time, their faces covered in concern.

Uh oh. This doesn't look good, thought Liv.

"Liv. What is this?" Mrs. Gordon put the phone up to Liv's eyes. Finn's adorable, bubble-covered face looked back at hers.

Liv's first thought was, *30 likes? Yes!!* But then she realized she might be in trouble. She tried to explain, "Oh, um, Finn just looked so cute, and I really wanted my friends to see him. All of my friends can post on Insta. It's not fair that I can't!"

"Peanut, it's not about it being fair. We made a rule that you could look but not post. And you broke the rule," said Mr. Gordon. "We need to know we can trust you and the more we can trust you the more privileges you'll get on your phone."

Then her dad said the most dreadful thing

ever: "So your mom and I are trying to decide whether you should still be allowed to go to the show tomorrow."

"No! No! I'm so sorry, Mom and Dad," Liv whispered on the verge of tears.

"I'm sorry, Liv, but you knew the rules," her dad said.

Her parents told her they needed to think about it and would tell her in the morning.

"But a horse show isn't like a soccer game," Liv said. "You can't just not go at the last minute. I'm entered in my classes and Finn is all set to go."

"It may not be a soccer game but we can still decide not to go," her father said.

Liv knew arguing might only make it worse. She headed to bed that night feeling nervous about everything. Nervous she wouldn't show. Nervous she would show. She had a difficult time falling asleep, tossing and turning and checking the clock. Time crawled by: 10:24 . . . 11:13 . . . 12:01 . . .

Sleep finally came. She dreamed that the horse trailer arrived at the horse show. But Finn wasn't on it. She had no pony to ride! She looked to the sky, where she saw Finn, floating around covered in sparkles, blowing bubbles down toward her face out of his nostrils. He looked at her and to her amazement, he opened his mouth and spoke to her, "Why aren't you at the show?"

CHAPTER EIGHT

MISCHIEF MAKER

L iv woke up with a start. Had she slept through her alarm? She rolled over. 5:02am. Phew. A half hour early. She yawned, rubbed her eyes, and then remembered last night. She wondered if her parents had made a decision.

She padded anxiously down the hall and slipped into her parents' bedroom. Her dad was already in the shower. Her mom was slowly waking up. Liv gently got on the bed and curled up next to her mom.

"Hi, baby," said Mrs. Gordon. Her voice was groggy.

"Mommy, I'm so sorry about the picture."

"I know, I know." Her mom's eyes opened and she looked right at Liv. "I think we were too hard on you last night. Your dad and I talked after you fell asleep. You can still do the show today."

Liv jumped up and twirled on the mattress before crashing back down on her mom with a big hug and a kiss.

An hour later, Liv arrived at the barn and quickly found Gemma. "You are not going to believe it," she said dramatically. "I almost missed the horse show because of my Insta post!"

Liv explained what had happened.

Gemma frowned. "Geez. Sorry! I had no idea. I shouldn't have made you post it."

"It's not your fault. It was my choice. Anyway,

whatever," Liv said before changing the subject. "Have you been by Finn's stall yet?"

Gemma hadn't, and she needed to go get Chewy ready. Meanwhile, Liv was dreading a big brown patch all over Finn's hind-end. Thankfully, he was very clean. Just a tiny brown smudge. Liv rubbed it off with a rag and water.

As Liv got Finn ready to go on the horse trailer, she heard a voice outside of his stall. "Look at this ridiculously adorable pony? I could just eat him up! He's too cute. Gemma, come introduce me!" Liv looked up and immediately recognized the *BEST.AUNT.EVER.*

*A*untie Mimi showed herself into Finn's stall and said, "You must be Liv! And this must be the famous fuzzy Finn!"

Mimi was holding a sleepy Jazz in one arm. She began hugging Finn's face with the other arm.

Liv could tell Mimi was a horse-person. Her purse was made out of the same plaid fabric as a horse blanket. Her belt-latch was shaped like a miniature silver horse bit. When she turned around, Liv was even surprised that sparkly rhinestones were studded onto her blue jeans, a horse shoe on each rear pocket.

Before they could talk, Kelly walked with purpose down the aisle and announced, "Let's get the horses loaded on the trailer!"

Twenty minutes later, the team from Mangrove Equestrian pulled out of the driveway in a caravan of cars and the horse trailer.

Gemma and Auntie Mimi began excitedly talking about everything horses the entire way. Jazz cooed and called out "PO-PO" every time she heard them say the word "pony." Gemma loved that her aunt had ridden in horse shows when she was a kid. She understood all about it.

Liv's ride was quieter. Her parents weren't

as knowledgeable about horses. She sat and listened to music. She looked for alligators sunning along the canals, but it was still too cold out that early in the morning. Even though she should have felt relaxed, Liv felt herself grow more tense with every minute of the drive.

*

The Mangrove caravan arrived at the horse show. Lots of horse trailers and cars were loosely lined up in a large grass field. Around them was a bustle of activity. Horses being groomed and saddled. Loose dogs of many varieties running around. Riders hustling to get show clothes on properly. Several sand arenas with horses having practice rides.

All the way across the field was an oval-shaped sand ring with a freshly painted white fence circling it. Liv could see a shed structure next to the ring. The judge would sit there during the long show day, no doubt grateful for some shade while evaluating the competitors.

The Gordons pulled their car next to where Mimi had parked the Shu-Risso's car. Before the girls even got out, Mimi burst out from the driver's seat. She spread her arms wide, sniffed the air, and exclaimed with her trademark enormous smile, "Nothing like an early morning horse show! Smell the wonder, girls!"

Liv and Gemma looked at each other and laughed. The show did indeed have a unique smell. The morning dew mixed with horse breath, grass, and of course horse manure.

The horse show announcer's voice crackled over the PA system, "Attention exhibitors, our first class will begin in thirty minutes."

Liv's stomach was full of butterflies. She took a deep breath, but it didn't really help. Peering over to the horse trailer, she caught sight of Finn's face. His ears were pricked forward and he looked excited to be at a horse show.

All of the Mangrove riders would be in different classes, except for Liv and Gemma. Everyone who wasn't riding in their own class helped their barnmates get ready. Landon was riding in the first class for beginners. Liv and Gemma helped him get his pony, Junebug, ready.

Liv and Gemma were in the next class after Landon. As soon as Landon headed to the ring with Kelly, the girls got their own ponies prepared. Both ponies looked clean and spiffy. They had bright white saddle pads and gleaming bridles and saddles.

Gemma laughed and chatted as they got ready, but Liv grew quiet and serious. She began to feel the fears she had after her bad lesson. What if Finn wouldn't listen to her? What if she couldn't steer him? She really wanted to do a good job and thought she might feel embarrassed if she made a mistake.

"C'mon Liv, let's go get the boys warmed up," said Gemma.

They rode over to one of the practice rings filled with horses trotting and cantering in all directions. Kelly had to remind both girls to be careful in the busy practice ring. Liv remembered Kelly's advice about not becoming a "pony pancake" and used her voice to tell other riders where she was going.

Sometimes horses were skittish in a new setting and were likely to go too fast. Chewy didn't seem to be rattled at all, but Finn had a lot of energy.

"I know, Finn," Liv whispered. "I'm nervous, too."

Liv thought of Gemma's advice in their lesson and said to Finn, "We can do it!"

She gave him a pat, then rode him around until he seemed more relaxed.

Both riders began to take some jumps. It was their final practice before they would go into the show arena. Liv worked hard to get Finn relaxed. As soon as she turned him to a jump, he forgot everything and raced toward it, cutting the corner. *Oh no,* thought Liv. It felt just like their bad lesson, but even worse. How would she ever make it around a course?

If Liv thought things were bad, Gemma was about to get a surprise from Chewy. Sometimes Chewy saved his best mischief for the worst moment. As she cantered around the corner, Chewy spotted a balloon at the nearby food truck. Chewy knew it was too far away to hurt him, but it still seemed like a fun reason to launch a buck!

Chapter Nine

Perfect Unicorns

"CHEWYYYYYY . . ." Kelly growled from the center of the warm-up ring. "Hold on, Gemma!"

Kelly watched as Chewy dropped his nose to the dirt and launched his bottom into the air.

Gemma was pitched forward onto his neck. She lost both stirrups, but she wrapped her legs and arms as tightly as she could around him.

As quickly as it happened, it was over. Chewy stood still, his head lazily cocked toward Kelly, who was jogging over to them. Thankfully,

Gemma was still aboard Chewy, lying on her belly on his neck.

"You okay?" Kelly asked with concern.

"Yeah, I'm fine." Gemma hoisted herself off his neck and back into the saddle.

"Phew. Well, I'm glad he got that out of his system. Better out here than in the show ring," Kelly said. "Now, give him a BIG kick and make him work extra hard from now on."

Gemma was rattled for a moment, but she took the mishap in good humor and was soon laughing about it. Another tale to add to the legend of Chocolate Charm. That was Chewy's official show name.

After the girls finished warming up, they pulled alongside each other by the show ring.

"You ready for this?" Gemma asked Liv.

"YOLO!" Liv tried to make a joke, but it fell flat. Her voice was a little shaky from nerves. "I didn't feel like I got Finn's attention in the warm-up. He's not listening when I ask him to wait before turning. So I don't know if we can do it."

"At least you can trust he won't buck!" Gemma laughed.

Liv did feel relieved about this. Finn was too eager sometimes, but he was also really reliable.

Just then, Auntie Mimi came over. She parked Jazz in the stroller a few feet away, and then wedged herself in between the two ponies. She draped her arms over each pony and said brightly, "How are my little winners?"

"Good," both girls said at the same time.

Mimi looked at Liv and could see she was tense and asked why. Liv explained her problem with Finn.

Mimi furrowed her brow, deep in thought. "You know, I had a pony like Finn once. And my trainer taught me a trick. He told me that I should pick a spot on the ring's outer fence, and then I should focus on riding to that spot. Once I got there, then I could look to the jump and turn. Somehow that helped a lot."

Kelly had walked up. "That's great advice, Mimi."

Kelly and Mimi had competed against each other when they were teenagers. They rode at different barns, and had both won many big championships. Kelly grew up and became a professional horse trainer. Mimi had decided to work as a curator for the United States Museum of Art and ride as a hobby.

"Alright, I'll take it from here," said Kelly.

She gave the girls some final pointers. "Gemma, remember Chewy likes to get lazy. You can't let him slow down. And for heaven's sake, when you go past the food truck, make sure he doesn't look over at the balloon!"

Gemma smiled, but started to feel a little bit jittery.

"And Liv, try to stay calm and relaxed. Trust Finn. He will always jump, no matter what. Remember you're the boss—he has to do what you tell him."

Landon was done showing, so he came along with a rag to help Liv and Gemma do a last-second cleaning. He wiped off the dirt from the girls' boots and cleaned the slime from the ponies' mouths. He gave them each a shy smile before disappearing into the crowd to watch.

They were ready to show!

＊

The announcer called out, "Next to go is Silver Finch and Olivia Gordon, followed by Chocolate Charm and Gemma Shu-Risso."

Liv wished she could watch Gemma go first. But the order-of-go was set.

She squeezed her legs and walked Finn toward the ring.

Even though Gemma loved winning, she also wanted her new friend to do well. She urgently whispered to Liv, "Remember to pick a spot on the rail and don't turn until you reach that spot."

"Got it," Liv said.

Liv stopped next to Kelly just before entering the ring. Kelly patted Finn on the shoulder and chirped, "Give him a smart ride out there. And have fun!"

Not all trainers told their riders to have fun. Kelly did it every time one of her riders went into the ring. Liv also remembered what Kelly had said in her lesson. *Smart girls are stable.* It helped Liv feel more confident.

As soon as she and Finn entered the ring, everything went silent. Liv was surprised because she felt calm and light. She didn't feel nervous anymore. Finn's canter felt magical. He seemed to float above the ground. For a split-second, Liv thought he'd literally turned into a real-life finch. No wonder he was named after a little bird!

As she approached the first corner, she remembered Mimi's advice. She picked her first spot along the outer fence. She focused hard and kicked Finn toward that spot. Instead of turning his head to try and see the jump too soon, Finn kept his sights straight ahead. Liv was thrilled that he listened. They came around the first corner in perfect form!

The rest of the course passed quickly. Liv could hardly believe it. She forgot to keep Finn straight in one place, but overall they had smooth jumps.

Kelly and the Mangrove crew were clapping and whooping as Liv came out of the ring.

"Great ride, Liv!" Kelly said. "And wow, I love

this pony. I swear he knows when he's showing. He's always perfect."

Mr. and Mrs. Gordon were standing nearby. Liv knew it was a relief for them to hear that. They had been unsure about buying a pony, and Kelly had to help them understand Finn was worth it. Now it was clear the Gordons had made a good decision. Liv leaned down, hugged Finn, and gave him a big kiss on the neck.

Gemma walked by and said, "I told you so."

"Told me what?"

"That you were lucky to have Finn!"

Gemma grinned. Liv remembered Gemma had said that when they first met.

"You're right! Well, now it's your turn. You're gonna kill it with Chewy," Liv said.

Gemma and Chewy swaggered into the ring. They had won lots of blue ribbons last year and she was really hoping to win another one, especially for her Auntie Mimi. She was grateful

Mimi had traveled so far and Gemma wanted to make her proud.

As she trotted Chewy, she caught sight of the awards table just outside the ring. It was filled with ribbons in a rainbow of bright colors: blue, red, yellow, white, pink, and green. Shiny silver and gold trophies topped with miniature horse figurines glinted in the sunshine.

Then she saw it—one of the special stuffed-animal sharks! Bright blue and teal striped with a gray belly. She was already dreaming of what it would be like to win it. But she would need to do well at all four Shark Island horse shows this year.

"Okay, Mr. Chewy, let's do this!" She gritted her teeth and squeezed Chewy's side. He was a little slow to get going. But then again, he always was. Gemma never lost her focus and kept him galloping forward throughout the course.

When she finished, Kelly gave a low whistle.

Gemma knew Kelly did that only for really good courses.

The girls hopped off their ponies and waited to hear the results. The Gordons and Mimi came over to hug the girls.

"Mimi, do you have my phone? We gotta take a selfie for Insta," said Gemma.

Mimi dug around her purse and pulled out the phone and handed it over.

As Gemma held up the phone, Liv looked to her parents, unsure of whether that would be okay. Without a word, Mrs. Gordon smiled and nodded.

Liv was relieved.

Auntie Mimi stepped in front of the girls and their ponies and started clucking and waving her hands, trying to get the ponies to put their ears forward. At just the right moment, Gemma snapped the picture.

Just then, the announcer's voice sounded

across the show grounds. "We have the results of our class." He first read a name the girls didn't recognize, then continued, "In second place is Chocolate Charm and Gemma Shu-Risso."

Liv turned to Gemma and exclaimed, "Awesome! You deserved it."

Gemma was excited. She knew this would earn her points toward that year-end award and one of the stuffed-animal sharks.

"In third place is Silver Finch and Olivia Gordon."

A wave of relief washed over Liv. She had won her first ribbon with Finn, and it was a pretty yellow ribbon. Most of all she was proud that she and Finn had improved together. They were learning to be a good team.

✻

Late that afternoon, the Mangrove group arrived back at the barn. Everyone felt tired, but it was important to take good care of the horses. They unloaded the ponies from the trailer, and tucked them into their stalls for the night. Dinner was a special bran-mash made with warm water that the ponies loved.

As soon as they were finished, Gemma sat down on her tack trunk to rest. Liv walked over, rubbing her sleepy blue eyes.

"Don't yawn, it's contagious," Liv said.

Gemma promptly yawned, and then Liv did, too.

They smiled and Liv put her arm around Gemma. "I'm glad we're friends."

"Me too. I can't wait to hang out more at the barn together," said Gemma.

"And go to more horse shows," said Liv.

The thought still made her a little uptight, but she knew they would have a lot of fun. She was looking forward to their next adventure together.

"Hey! I never put up that pic on Insta!" Gemma said suddenly. She pulled out her phone and selected the pic of both girls and their ponies from earlier that day. She picked a filter that made it look like they were standing in the warm light of a sunset. "What should I write as the caption?"

"How about 'two peas in a pod'?" offered Liv.

"Hmm. Nah, something else . . ." Gemma tapped in *pony pals #perfectponies* then erased it. It always took a few tries to get just the right feel. She tried one more time.

perfect unicorns & my #barnBFF

She added two unicorn emojis and two red hearts. Liv and Gemma looked at each other and grinned.

Just right.

Turn the page for a sneak preview of Book 2 in the #BarnBFF series:

Hard to Catch

Bonus Excerpt

#BarnBFF: Book 2
Hard to Catch

by Kim Ablon Whitney & Caraneen Smith

Chapter One

Gemma Shu-Risso stared at the clock in her school classroom. She wished the minute hand would move faster. Just fifteen more minutes until she could go to Mangrove Equestrian Center and see her beautiful chocolate-colored pony, Chewy.

She twiddled with her long, dark hair as her science teacher continued the lesson about how thunderstorms form. "So as the warm air rises into the clouds, it gets cooler and the moisture in the air condenses into rain drops."

Gemma's father was a doctor and loved science, but it wasn't her favorite subject. Still, it was a good topic for the girls at Hickory Bay Academy. The school was in Palm Palisades, Florida and thunderstorms rolled through frequently.

Gemma was calm by nature, but she didn't like lightning and thunder. The loud boom from a nearby thunderbolt always startled her.

Finally the school bell rang.

"Don't forget—tornado drill tomorrow," the teacher said as the students gathered their backpacks.

"Yay!" someone said behind Gemma.

Gemma and her classmates liked tornado drills. It was awkward going into the hallway and crouching into a ball on the floor, but it was better than having to do schoolwork!

Gemma said goodbye to her friends and rushed out the door thinking about Chewy's adorable face. He had a crooked white blaze and velvet-soft nose.

Gemma's mother waited in her car at the curb.

"Hi, Gem! What did you have for lunch today?" Her mother always asked her what she had for lunch. Gemma thought it was a little odd, but Mrs. Shu-Risso simply figured it was an easier question to answer than, "How was school?"

"Grilled cheese," Gemma replied. "You wouldn't believe what happened in the cafeteria. My friend spilled milk all over the table. It was a mess. Everyone helped clean it up, though. And I grabbed an extra granola bar to share with Chewy."

"He'll love that!" Mrs. Shu-Risso said. Mrs. Shu-Risso worked in human resources at a local technology company. After her recent divorce, she started working full-time again. She negotiated with the company so she could work from home part of the day. That way she could still pick up Gemma from school.

"I'm glad you can drive me to the barn again," Gemma said. During her parents' divorce, things had been a little crazy. Sometimes neither of her parents could pick her up and Gemma had to get rides with her friends.

One time her riding trainer, Kelly Van Beek, even picked her up at school and brought her to Mangrove Equestrian. It was nice of Kelly, because she was always so busy teaching. Luckily the farm was just across town from Hickory Bay Academy.

"Our chats on the way to the barn are a highlight of my day," Mrs. Shu-Risso said. "Oh, I almost forgot to remind you—today is your dentist appointment. I have to pick you up early."

Gemma groaned. "I hate the dentist."

"No one likes the dentist, silly! But you want to have teeth when you're 90 so you can still chew your food," her mother joked. "You'll need to ride fast. I'll pick you up in an hour and a half."

"That's not nearly enough time!" Gemma protested.

"It is if you don't dawdle and chit-chat with your friends, or play on your phone. Just focus on riding and caring for Chewy."

Gemma knew her mom was right, but she was still annoyed that the dentist appointment would cut into her barn time.

Gemma looked forward to going to Mangrove Equestrian Center more than anything. Chewy was like a furry friend, Kelly was like a second mom, and she always loved hanging out with her *#BarnBFF*, Liv Gordon.

As they drove along, Gemma scrunched up

her face in disgust, took a selfie and posted it to her Instagram, *#dentisttoday #UGHHHHH!!!* A moment later, Liv posted a comment with a screaming-face emoji, and Gemma chuckled.

Mrs. Shu-Risso pulled the car into the dirt driveway at Mangrove Equestrian. Palm trees lined the driveway and at the far end stood the big red barn. Gemma said goodbye and hopped out of the car.

Liv hadn't gotten to the barn yet. Liv went to Palm Palisades Elementary. Even though her school got out earlier than Gemma's, her parents liked her to go home before riding. She had a snack and changed clothes before going to the barn.

Gemma changed into her riding pants and headed to Chewy's stall. There was a beautiful red ribbon hanging on the door from their last horse show together. Gemma smiled to herself with pride.

Gemma noticed the latch was undone and the stall was empty. Most of the horses were inside, enjoying some shade from the afternoon sun. Gemma wondered if Chewy had escaped. When he was younger, he had figured out how to open the latch with his wiggly lips. He hadn't done that in a few years.

She was about to go look for him as the barn manager, Alonso Sosa, walked in. He was like everyone's favorite grandpa, always cheerful and friendly. His short, wavy hair was streaked with dark gray and white. His face was weathered, but the crinkled skin showed that he had spent most of his life smiling.

"Hi, Miss Gemma!" Alonso said. He was originally from Argentina and made the word "Miss" sound like *Meeeees*. He continued, "You looking for Chewy?"

"Yep!" Gemma hoped Alonso would say Chewy was getting new horse shoes. Instead

Alonso said just what Gemma did not want to hear.

"Chewy is in the field."

Gemma's shoulders slumped. She didn't have much time and it would take longer to walk out to the pasture. Chewy also loved to roll in the dirt patch next to the gate. If he was dirty, it would take Gemma forever to get him clean.

Worst of all, Chewy was sometimes hard to catch. He had been in the Shu-Risso family for years, but no one had been able to figure out why sometimes he wouldn't let anyone catch him. One time Gemma's older sister, Skylar, had spent two whole hours trying to catch him.

Gemma headed toward the fields behind the barn where Chewy and a few other ponies were turned out. She saw Chewy at the far side of the field. His coat glistened in the sun and he looked clean. That was a relief.

Even though it had been a dry spell in Florida,

the farm had large sprinklers that shot water across the fields overnight. That meant the grass was lush and green. It was delicious for Chewy to graze on, which also meant he might not want to come in.

Gemma entered the pasture, clutching Chewy's royal blue lead rope. Chewy and the other ponies lifted their heads and looked at her.

Gemma called in a happy, high pitched voice: "Chewy! Hi, Chewy boy! How's my cute pony?"

Chewy recognized Gemma's voice. He kept his eyes trained on her while she walked toward him. The other ponies went back to grazing. Gemma hoped he'd take a step toward her, but he didn't budge.

Gemma was close to him now. She crinkled the wrapper to the granola bar she had snagged from school. Chewy flicked an ear and Gemma broke off a piece of the treat. She held out her hand. Chewy's soft nose tickled Gemma's fingers as he scooped the granola bar into his mouth.

Phew, thought Gemma. He wasn't going to run away today. Chewy's ears were floppy now, which meant he was relaxed. Gemma gave him a pat. She brought the lead rope to his head and went to attach it to his halter.

He took a step back.

Gemma tensed. She rushed to attach the clasp to his halter, but Chewy spun away and galloped off at full speed.

"Noooooo!" Gemma's heart sank. "I'll never catch him now!"

❊

About the Authors

Kim Ablon Whitney is a USEF 'R' judge and the author of many other books about horses. She lives with her family in Newton, Massachusetts.

Caraneen Smith created and runs the popular website Bigeq.com. A lifelong equestrian, she owns two horses, Lucky Duck and Coco Twist. She lives in Hingham, Massachusetts.

Thank you to our families and friends!

Made in the USA
Middletown, DE
20 July 2019